P9-DGQ-876

# THE FIREFIGHTERS

Sue Whiting ILLUSTRATED BY Donna Rawlins

CANDLEWICK PRESS
CAMBRIDGE, MASSACHUSETTS

# BRIIIIIING! BRIIIIIING!

the alarm sounds.

"Quick!" I say. "Coats and boots!"

"Hats, too," says Mia.

"Hurry, Mrs. Iverson," says Jack.

"There's a fire!"

We're playing firefighters. We're just like the **REAL** ones.

"Climb on board," I say.

"Squeeze in, Mrs. Iverson," says Mia.

"The door won't close."

"Siren's on," says Jack. "Let's **GO, GO, GO!**"

We're in our fire engines.

They're just like the **REAL** ones.

# WEEE-OOO! WEEE-OOO! WEEE-OOO!

the siren yells.

"Quick!" I say. "Around the corner."

"And up the hill," says Mia.

"Then onto Drury Lane," says Mrs. Iverson.

"No!" shouts Jack. "That's the wrong way!"

Silly Mrs. Iverson.

We rush out the door.

# WEEE-OOO! WEEE-OOO! WEEE-OOO!

We tear past the climbing fort and tunnel.

We dash past the sandbox.

# WEEE-OOO! WEEE-OOO! WEEE-OOO!

Everyone stops and stares, but we don't have time to wave.

Our fire engines are fast and noisy—just like the **REAL** ones.

"There's the fire," I say. "Quick! Pull over."

"Connect the hoses," says Mia.

"We have to hurry," says Mrs. Iverson,

"or Lulu's Ice Creamery will go up too!"

"This could get dangerous,"
says Jack. "Be careful."

The fire is hot. The flames crack and
pop and tickle the sky.
The smoke is really stinky.
"Oxygen masks," says Mrs. Iverson.
Good thinking. We pull on our masks.

Mia and Jack hold one hose.

Mrs. Iverson and I hold the other.

Water shoots out and blasts the fire.

whoosh! whoosh! whoosh!

We're firefighters, brave and strong—just like the **REAL** ones.

"Fire's out," I say.

"We did it!" says Mia.

"And we saved Lulu's,"
   says Mrs. Iverson.

"Good job, everyone,"
says Jack.

We flop to the ground—tired and dirty.

Then . . . **WEEE-OOO! WEEE-OOO! WEEE-OOO!** What's that?

**WEEE-OOO! WEEE-OOO! WEEE-OOO!** A siren?

"Look!" I say.

"Wow," says Mia.

"Too noisy," yells Jack,
 covering his ears.

"Surprise!" says Mrs. Iverson.

It's a fire engine. **A REAL ONE.**

The fire engine drives into the yard

and stops right outside our classroom.

The doors swing open,

and out step two firefighters.

**REAL ONES!**

Mrs. Iverson gets us to sit in the shade.

The firefighters tell us stories about fighting fires

and rescuing people from burning buildings.

It sounds exciting — and scary.

They tell us that if there is a fire in a building we're in,

we should get down low and *GO, GO, GO!*

"Let's pretend,"
   says one of the firefighters.

"Oh, no!" shouts the other.
"There's smoke!
   There must be a fire."

We're not silly.
We know what to do.
We get down low and
*GO, GO, GO!*

"We're good at pretending,"
   I tell the firefighters.
"We can see that!"
   they say.

When we are all sitting down again,
one of the firefighters says,
"Would anyone like to climb
on board the fire truck?"

"YES!" we shout.
And we do.
Three at a time.

The fire engine is big and red and shiny.

There are dials and buttons everywhere.

Mia and I take turns switching on the siren.

Jack speaks into the radio.

"Don't worry. We're on our way," he says.

I love it.

I **REALLY** do.

"You know, we're firefighters too,"
   I tell the firefighters.
"Just not the **REAL** ones like you.
   Not *yet*!"

For Samantha, Hayden, and
all the crazy cats in 1/2 Red,
even Ms. P.
S. W.

For Mia and Henry Callum
D. R.

Text copyright © 2008 by Sue Whiting
Illustrations copyright © 2008 by Donna Rawlins

First U.S. edition 2008

Library of Congress Cataloging-in-Publication Data is available.

Library of Congress Catalog Card Number 2007051895

ISBN 978-0-7636-4019-4

10 9 8 7 6 5 4 3 2          JAN 0 9 2009

Printed in Singapore

This book was typeset in Abadi and Machine.
The illustrations were done in acrylic.

Candlewick Press
2067 Massachusetts Avenue
Cambridge, Massachusetts 02140

visit us at www.candlewick.com